British 'Tommy'
1914

French 'Poilu'
1914

British soldier
World War II

American G.I.
World War II

Russian soldier
World War II

French soldier
World War II

Today, all modern armies look much alike.

to teachers and parents

This is a LADYBIRD LEADER book, one of a series specially produced to meet the very real need for carefully planned *first information books* that instantly attract enquiring minds and stimulate reluctant readers.

The subject matter and vocabulary have been selected with expert assistance, and the brief and simple text is printed in large, clear type.

Children's questions are anticipated and facts presented in a logical sequence. Where possible, the books show what happened in the past and what is relevant today.

Special artwork has been commissioned to set a standard rarely seen in books for this reading age and at this price.

Full colour illustrations are on all 48 pages to give maximum impact and provide the extra enrichment that is the aim of all Ladybird Leaders.

A Ladybird Leader

soldiers

written by John West

illustrated by Frank Humphris

Ladybird Books Loughborough

Soldiers of Ancient Egypt 2000 — 1100 BC

The soldiers had spears with bronze tips.
Their arrows had tips of bone or flint.
Shields were made of wood and leather.
A king rode into battle in his chariot.

Assyrian soldiers
1100 — 600 BC

The Assyrian armies were very strong.

They defeated many other countries.

The soldiers had helmets made of bronze.

Some wore armour
made of metal strips sewn on leather.

Swords and dagger

Leg armour

Hoplites

Greek soldiers 650 — 300 BC

Greek soldiers were called hoplites.
They wore bronze helmets,
breastplates and leg armour.
Their shields were large and round.

Greek helmets

Charioteers

Some spears were 7 metres long.
These soldiers had to pay for
their own spears, swords, daggers
and armour.
Poor men could not become hoplites.

King Darius of Persia 521 — 486 BC

King Darius ruled the Persian Empire.
He wanted to rule the world.
His army was said to be unbeatable,
but it was defeated by the Greeks.

Darius had a bodyguard of 10,000 men.
They had spears, bows and arrows
and were richly dressed.

Fighting men of the Holy Land

Long before the birth of Christ,
men like these fought
in the Holy Land.

Warriors
of the Iron Age
550 BC — 50 AD

During the Iron Age in Europe,
swords, spears and helmets
were of iron.

Iron is much harder than bronze.

Tribesmen fought men of other tribes.

There were no paid soldiers.

The Roman Army
100 BC — 400 AD

Roman soldiers were very well trained;
they were the finest of their time.

They were also very well armed.
They could march 25 kilometres
in four hours.

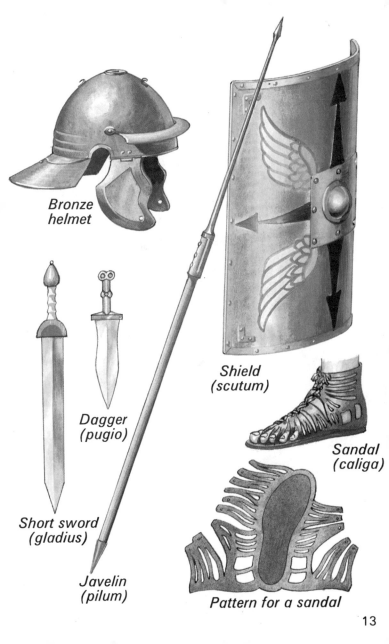

Bronze helmet

Short sword (gladius)

Dagger (pugio)

Javelin (pilum)

Shield (scutum)

Sandal (caliga)

Pattern for a sandal

13

Officer   *Centurion*   *Standard bearer*

A legion was made up of 6,000 men.
A centurion was in charge of 100 men.
The standard bearer led an attack.

a Roman fortress

Roman cavalry

Horn blower

The Romans defeated the Greeks.
They also conquered France, Britain,
Spain, Palestine and North Africa.

The Gauls

These were tribesmen in Gaul (France).
They were conquered by the Roman army
When the Romans defeated them,
they became part of the Roman army.

The Huns

Between 400 — 500 AD, the Huns swarmed across Europe.

Under their leader, Attila, they were hated and feared.

The Battle of Hastings

The Normans invaded England in 1066.

The Saxons had few archers
and no cavalry (soldiers on horseback).

William the Conqueror gave land
and other rewards to his soldiers.

19

The Crusades (Holy Wars)

From 1096 to 1291 AD there were 'Holy Wars' to capture Jerusalem from the Turks. Crusaders went from many parts of Europe.

They were Christians.

Turks were Muslims.

A suit of armour
weight about 25 kg

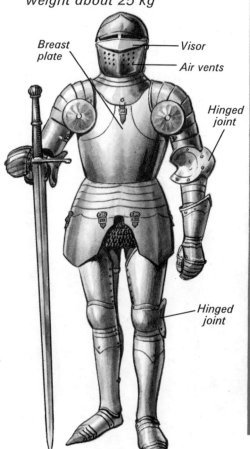

Breast plate

Visor

Air vents

Hinged joint

Hinged joint

Helmet

Gauntlet

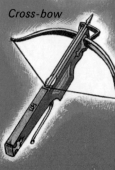

Cross-bow

By 1430, armour was much better.

It was not so heavy.

Thin, special steel was being used.

A knight could move more easily.

The long-bow and the cross-bow

Long-bow

Cross-bow

The arrow from a long-bow
could go through armour.

It could kill at about 200 metres.

The cross-bow was slower to use.

Early cannon

1450

This man is using an early hand-gun

The invention of gunpowder changed the way soldiers fought. Armour no longer saved them. Cannon balls could knock down city walls!

1500

1450

The first cannon were made in 1326 AD.
Some blew themselves up!
A cannon ball could weigh 340 kg.
By 1500, cannon were being moved
on wheels.

Royal Marine cap

British and French cuff

Light Dragoon helmet

British Infantry 1751

French Horse-soldier 1750

Prussian Grenadier 1755

After cannon, hand-guns were made.

Muskets and pistols replaced long-bows

Soldiers were grouped into regiments.

Flintlock musket 'Brown Bess'

Flintlock pistol

French Infantry 1760

Prussian 5th Dragoon 1770

Royal Fusilier 1789

From 1680, coloured uniforms were worn.

Most French soldiers wore white coats, the Germans blue, and the English red.

Joining an army

Armies grew bigger. More men were needed. Some were tricked into joining

Sometimes they were dragged away after they had been made drunk.

A soldier's life was very hard.

The men who made America a free nation

These soldiers were American settlers, not trained soldiers.

Between 1771 and 1783, they fought and beat trained soldiers of the British army.

Napoleon Bonaparte

Napoleon was one of the greatest generals in history.

His mighty French armies fought in Spain, Egypt, Italy, Holland and Russia.

Russian soldiers and the Russian winter destroyed Napoleon's 'Grand Army'.

After his retreat from Moscow in 1812, only 45,000 men (out of 300,000) got home.

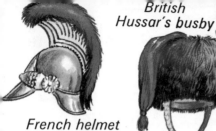

British
Hussar's busby

French helmet

French cap

The Duke of Wellington at the Battle of Waterloo

Napoleon formed a new army.

This won many victories
before it was beaten
by Russians and Germans.

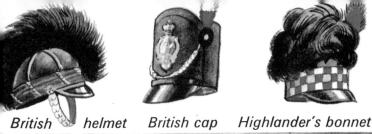

British helmet   *British cap*   *Highlander's bonnet*

Later, he formed yet another army.

In 1815, he was finally beaten at Waterloo by a German army and British army under the Duke of Wellington.

The Charge of the Light Brigade

In the Crimean War, British cavalry bravely charged the Russian guns.

The British lost nearly half the men who were in this charge.

All wars are cruel and wasteful.

Many people die or are crippled.

These men were on the winning side,
but afterwards could live only by begging.

African warriors

These were Zulu warriors
of 100 years ago.

They conquered a large part of Africa
and were feared by other tribes.

Japanese Samurai 1600

Somali Dervish 1890

Mexican 1900

Pathan (India) 1900

Soldiers of other lands

Not all soldiers had regimental uniforms.

These were fighting men too.

They were just as brave.

The American Civil War 1861—1865

Americans of the Northern States
fought Americans of the Southern State

The bitter struggle lasted 4 years.
The North won. They had better weapons
and more money to buy them.

The North American Indians

100 years ago, North American Indian fought to stop white Americans from taking their lands.

The white men had more and better guns, so the Indians lost.

Soldiers of India

These soldiers of India
were wonderful fighters.

The men on horseback
were Bengal lancers.

The soldier with a rifle was in
a famous Gurkha regiment.

New uniforms

Portuguese
1890

French
1890

Japanese
1900

Prussian
1870

British
1895

American
1899

In 1870, the German army
was one of the best in the world.

The armies of some other countries
copied the German uniforms.

Some also copied the spiked helmet.

The first 'khaki' uniforms

In 1899, British soldiers in Africa wore khaki coats, not red.

'Khaki' means 'dust-coloured'.

Khaki uniforms are not so easily seen by an enemy.

The First World War

From 1914 to 1918, many countries were at war.

It is often called 'The Great War'.

8,000,000 men died. Many more were wounded.

Tanks and aircraft were used in battle for the first time.
For safety, soldiers wore steel helmets.
They dug trenches and lived in them.
They climbed out to attack.

The Second World War 1939—1945

Armies moved swiftly into battle
in trucks, tanks and aircraft.
Some soldiers were landed in gliders
or dropped by parachute.

Special ships quickly landed men, tanks, trucks and guns on enemy beaches.

47

Modern airborne soldiers

Today, helicopters can take men,
guns and trucks into battle
in any part of the world.

War in the desert

War in the snow

War in the jungle

Modern soldiers
are trained to fight anywhere.

In the past, soldiers fought other soldiers
In war today, nobody is safe.
Any man, woman or child can be killed,
injured or made homeless.

Military rockets can travel
many thousands of kilometres.
Even the largest cities
could be destroyed instantly.

Index